SECONDHAND SINGULARITY

RACHEL AUKES

SECONDHAND SPACEMAN SERIES

1. Secondhand Spaceman
2. Secondhand Starship
3. Secondhand Singularity
4. Secondhand Smuggler

SECONDHAND SINGULARITY
Secondhand Spaceman Series, Book 3

Waypoint Books LLC

Cover image includes elements created using Midjourney
Edited by Diane Bryant

Ebook ASIN: B0CMJK1RFP
Print ISBN: 978-1-956120-08-0

—————

Sign up for Rachel's newsletter to be the first to hear about
new releases and upcoming projects: www.rachelaukes.
com/join

For Brian, always.

CONTENTS

1. Tarkov the Most Impressive — 1
2. Hello, Goodbye — 13
3. Man Against the Machine — 22
4. Old Dogs, New Tricks — 31
5. Fortune Favors the Bold — 38
6. Now Would Be a Good Time to Take Up a New Sport — 47
7. Kindness is Contagious (and Deadly) — 52
8. The Old Banana Peel Trick — 64
9. With a Little Help From My Friends — 74

Continue Reading — 81
Also by Rachel Aukes — 83
About the Author — 85
Acknowledgments — 87

1 / TARKOV THE MOST IMPRESSIVE

Surprisingly, standup comedy clubs in space have much the same vibe as comedy clubs back on Earth. Both are dark, old, and smell of booze. Though, I'd give Terrans a thumbs-up in the comedy department. Every alien race has their own idea as to what's funny, and from all the aliens of various shapes and sizes I've come across so far, none have had a funny bone (some don't even have bones). Most were like Brits if you took away their sense of sarcasm. I'd sat through two acts tonight, and both were beyond painful to watch. I was still sitting there, making me wonder if I wasn't a masochist.

But I wasn't there for the entertainment—I was there on the job.

The next standup act was a female Floid. She was attractive, but that's to be expected for a Floid. Imagine a green-skinned alien babe with curves in all the right places. It's a race that is the alien version of Brazilians. They're all hot. Except Floids' hair looks like broccoli, though it works, oddly enough. Looking at her, it was safe to assume she'd be the crowd favorite tonight even if her jokes were the worst of the lot.

I, however, didn't plan on watching her performance. I stepped out and made my way down the hallway. I could get backstage without any sort of badge check, which shows just how low on the popularity scale these acts are. I think the entire audience was made up of friends or family… except for me, the lone repo man, of course.

I snuck in the Floid's dressing room and grabbed the biggest flower bouquet on her dressing table. I plucked off the card, tossed it over my shoulder, and then pulled out a card of my own and slid it into the card holder. The bouquet was so large that it was a bit difficult to hold with one arm since my prosthetic arm had a claw that tended to either grip things too hard and break them or too soft and drop them.

I carried that bouquet three doors down where I came to a sign that read, *Tarkov the Most Impressive*. My guess? He wasn't.

I knocked. "Delivery for Tarkov the Most Impressive."

A few seconds later, the door opened to reveal a Zyglar in a tuxedo. He was gray, almost fishlike in appearance with an oblong head, large black eyes, and huge finned ears. His nose consisted of two slits and his mouth was filled with piranha teeth. Otherwise, he bore a humanoid body shape. I work with two Zyglars on occasion. They're known for being business-savvy, but they're not known for their sense of humor. They're also not known for integrity. A rodent has more scruples than they do.

One perk of being a Terran in a galaxy of

aliens is that my race is one of the least intimidating of all races. We don't have horns, tusks, or claws. We really don't have any features that would scare anyone—Terrans are basically the teddy bears of the universe. Being a Terran comes in handy on repo jobs. Most folks tend to underestimate me, and I like it that way.

Tarkov showed no fear whatsoever at seeing me, and his black eyes homed in on the bouquet with both surprise and doubt. He must've been a *really* bad comedian.

"The card's inside," I said, assuming he had a universal translator.

I did not have a universal translator. I had a Shrike. He's a technologically based symbiont goo that made himself at home inside my body. He can translate a lot of languages—at least every single language I've come across so far. But he's only *half* as good as a universal translator because while Shrike instantly translates in my brain, he hasn't figured out yet how to tell me what to say in the right language. Essentially, I'm still stuck with my native English tongue, which absolutely no one in space speaks since Terrans aren't even considered an interstellar race yet.

Tarkov plucked out the card and read it. I'd written it in the universal language (thanks to my ship computer's help), so I didn't need to see it to know what it said.

I'm your biggest fan. Call me for a good time. Love, Lina. 9A9GJ897-4234G.

When Fetch told me what to write, I thought she was lacking in the creativity department, but she was convinced that it would work just fine on a Zyglar. Since my ship's computer has a few hundred years' more experience in dealing with aliens than I do, I went with it. And, by the look on Tarkov's face and the blush in his big ears, it worked.

"I'll, uh, just set these on the table over there," I said.

He ignored me, already tapping in the digits in his armlet to place the call. I carried the bouquet into the dressing room. In the chair next to the table sat Mutzy, Tarkov's puppet (as he was a ventriloquist which made it all the more likely that he was the *worst* comedian scheduled to perform tonight).

"*Hello?*" a feminine voice answered through Tarkov's armlet speakers.

"Lina?" he asked, his voice quivering a bit.

"*Yes. Is this Tarkov the Impressive?*"

"No, this is Tarkov the *Most* Impressive." His chest puffed out. "And I received your bouquet."

"*I'm your biggest fan. You're so funny, and your ears are so sexy.*"

Tarkov took a seat and propped his feet up. "Tell me more, sweet ums."

Tarkov had no clue he was talking to Fetch, who was applying whatever wiles a ship computer has to keep him distracted. He was completely ensconced in his conversation. I grabbed Mutzy, and hustled out of the dressing room, closing the door quietly but quickly behind me. As soon as I was clear, I took off running to Satuza Station's docks.

Like all space waystations, it was a minimum ten-minute jog back from any social establishment to the docks, and Satuza Station was more spread out than most. From the outside, the station looked like a large dirty-white ball covered in small dirty-white balls (which reminded me of used cotton balls). The docks were located on the top and bottom of the station based on how the artificial gravity was set up. The comedy club was in one of those small balls. I'd parked in the nearest dock, but I still had to jog out of the little ball, down seven levels of the big ball, and halfway through the lower dock.

I was hoping Fetch could keep Tarkov distracted until I reached *Fetch*, my ship (I know, calling my ship computer the same name as my ship is lame, but since she's cool with it, I'm cool with it).

"Quit jostling me like a kid giving himself his first hand job," said a wry yet whiny masculine voice.

I stumbled and barely stopped myself from falling. I slowed enough to look down at the puppet in the crook of my arm. Its eyes were wide open and looking directly at me.

"Uh, did you talk to me?" I asked.

"Of course I did. That is, unless you're carrying another puppet in your pants," it said.

"But you're a puppet. How are you talking?"

"Because I'm a ventriloquist's puppet, you big dummy. Ironic, a puppet calling you a dummy, am I right?"

"Sure, whatever, but the ventriloquist is supposed to be doing the talking. That's how ventriloquists work."

"If they got any talent, yeah. But those who don't have the talent buy puppets with built-in voice modulators, like me."

Now that my shock had worn off, I began jogging again. "I figured Tarkov was bad, but I didn't realize he's a fraud."

"Oh, the thief's calling Tarkov a fraud. That's rich," Mutzy said.

"I'm not a thief. I'm a repo agent for 3S—Starshine Seizure Specialists. So, Tarkov's not just a fraud, he doesn't pay his bills," I said as I passed a couple who eyed me strangely for conversing with a puppet.

"I told him not to spend that last check on that cheap dock donkey, Harriet, but does he ever listen to me? No," Mutzy said.

"A dock donkey?"

"You know, hooker, prostitute, wh—"

"I get it," I said.

"Well, you asked." It gave me the side-eye. "You know, they say you can tell a lot about a guy by the size of his ears. And yours are the smallest I've ever seen."

"Hey! You know, you're just being mean and not funny at all."

"You know what's funny? Your face," it said. "And your arm. What's up with that arm, anyway? It's like three sizes too big and looks like it's been spit out of the recycler because it was too ugly. Steal that arm, too, did ya?"

My prosthetic arm might not have been pretty, but it worked (mostly). "I bought it fair and square."

"Well, whatever you paid, you paid too much."

"Say one more thing, and I'm going to pop your head off," I said, snapping the claw at the end of my prosthetic.

"Thing," it said, just waiting for my response.

I moved my metal pincers toward its neck even though I had to slow my stride to do it.

"I bet you don't get paid if you damage me," Mutzy said.

Damn it if he wasn't right. "I'll might just get docked. You want to find out?"

It wisely didn't speak.

I reached the station's dock and hustled to my ship. *Fetch* was a cylindrical ship with angled sides rather than rounded like a lot of ships. Two engines stuck out from the rear sides of the ship with two smaller navigational engines placed on the top and bottom at the middle of the ship. Dark gray patches covered nearly the entire rusty brown hull. The hull hadn't been in *that* bad of shape when I patched it, but when I discovered that the material used on an old Dyson sphere did a bang-up job at fortifying *Fetch*'s hull, I covered everything I could. After all, every repo ticket tended to include trouble, free of charge.

The patches held pretty good even if they didn't look pretty. The only problem I'd had so far with them happened not long after I finished repairs. We'd just left a meeting with Jack, our GOD handler (trust me, you don't want to meet GOD), and one of the panels snapped off and smacked an engine. We were down for three days fixing that. Fortunately, just before that, I'd knocked a Calcar ship offline, and they were down a lot longer. Calcars are basically space orcs, so the more distance between them and me, the better. Especially since those particular Calcars were trying to kill me.

"You're taking me in *that*?" The puppet actually sounded afraid.

"Nope. You're getting dropped in a courier drone and shipped back, priority mail, to the bank," I said.

"You wouldn't dare stick me in one of those boxes. They don't even have cushioning!" Mutzy said.

I tapped the computer panel next to the airlock. The outer door opened, and I glanced over my shoulder. Even though I didn't see Tarkov, I hurried inside and closed the door. "How're we doing with Tarkov, Fetch?"

"I'm still talking to him. Amazing how stroking a Zyglar's ego can keep him distracted indefinitely. I think he'll miss his standup act if I keep talking." Fetch's voice sounded like that of a biker chick who smoked ten packs a day for twenty years. I didn't set her voice parameters—my dad did, and since *Fetch* was all I had left to remember him, I never changed her voice.

"Ego? You oughtta try stroking his ears," Mutzy blurted out.

"The puppet speaks?" Fetch asked.

"It speaks," I said.

And it annoys me. You should destroy it, Shrike said in my mind.

"We're not destroying anything," I said. "Fetch, prepare for launch."

"I'm already through the pre-launch sequence, and the flight plan's been approved. I advise you to ship the puppet at your earliest convenience as it seems Tsara's goons have entered the local quadrant."

"What? Why didn't you tell me?"

"I just did," she said.

Mutzy chuckled. "I like the broad. She's got

style. Keep me onboard, and I'll show her what it means to *turn on* a computer."

I just shook my head at Mutzy and hustled to the cargo hold. In the center sat a courier drone which looked like a missile but functioned more like a shipping box. Courier drones were the most popular form of shipping; there were so many out there, they even had their own spaceways allocated across the universe. That way, ships and drones didn't run the risk of colliding because collisions in space can really suck.

I popped open the lid to the drone and stuck the puppet inside.

"Whoa! Let's talk about this. No need to stuff me inside a box," Mutzy said.

"Sorry. You gotta go back to the bank. Tarkov missed a few too many payments, and they didn't think that was very funny." With that, I closed the cover and powered on the drone while Mutzy continued his ranting.

Code scrolled across the drone's screen. "I have control. The moment we are clear of the docks, I will open the cargo bay and deploy the courier. I recommend you make haste to the cockpit and secure yourself for launch," Fetch said.

"You don't need to tell me twice." I hustled, closing and sealing the door that separated the cargo bay from the rest of the ship and double-checked everything so that when Fetch decompressed the bay, I wouldn't die.

It didn't take long to reach the cockpit since the cargo bay made up over half of the ship. There, I buckled in just as the engines fired up and I felt the docking clamps release. To my right was a large round window—the only one on this level—and I decided to look out as Fetch navigated us out of Satuza Station's dock. It was a better view than all the system alerts flashing on-screen. My ship had the whole shebang of outdated systems, busted parts, glitches, and faulty wiring and the screen never let me forget it.

Enough problems that I'd come up with Rule Number Five of Space Travel: If your flight is going well, something is about to break.

Needless to say, my ship needed a little TLC.

But *Fetch* kept on flying, no matter what I put her through. And she did all the flying, too. Bioforms, like me, weren't allowed to handle flight controls since we aren't as precise as a computer. Plus, bioforms tend to make judgment calls, which always work in the movies but don't work out so well in real life. So, that leaves me riding along, looking pretty, while Fetch does all the work.

That's not to say I don't have my share of work, too. When I'm not working a ticket, I'm working my way through the ship's problem log, though I tend to call it a problem book because it's so long. Fetch doesn't find that as funny as I do.

"Where're those goons now, Fetch?" I asked.

"They're preparing to dock at Satuza Station. Fortunately, it appears they did not notice our departure," she replied.

"First good news I've heard all day." I leaned back and propped my feet on the console (which drives Fetch crazy). "This ticket's going in my memoir for sure. How many repo agents get to grab puppets, and raunchy puppets at that?"

"Your memoir will be a titillating read," Fetch said.

"You're being sarcastic, but that's okay. I know it's going to be a *great* read regardless of what you think." I considered something for a moment. "You know, after this ticket, we should have at least a week or two of down time. Maybe we should check out that new bar on Tzerina. I could get some writing done and also make a few extra bucks running something for Qualixs. What do ya think, Fetch?"

"I think any vacations will have to wait. Totty received the shipment scans and has already deposited payment for the annoying puppet."

Totty's my boss, and she's a dick. She looks like a giant purple jellybean, and all she cares about is making money. My dad had been forced into a contract with her to work as a repo agent. When he died, the contract rolled over to me (you can thank GOD for designing *inheritable* work contracts). Totty kidnapped me from campus and forced me to sign my dad's contract. And so now I have to work as a space repo man for Starshine Scizure Specialists for the next eighty-one years, eight months, and two weeks. Since then, I don't expect good news.

"What is this, Christmas?" I asked.

"I wouldn't celebrate too soon. Totty also sent details on the next ticket. It's a higher value ticket. A rogue mechanoid needs to be collected and returned to its corporation."

I shrugged. "That doesn't sound any harder than grabbing a puppet."

"This mechanoid is a security unit equipped with an arsenal of weaponry and fully programmed in a variety of combat tactics. It's an older model but still more than deadly enough in most situations."

I sighed. "Of course it is. Why're they sending me? I thought mechs can be recalled by their own corporation?"

"This particular unit removed both its tracker and control chip, which makes it a high-priority reclamation ticket. The corporation can't have one of their security units loose for liability risks... and it might be bad PR, of course."

"Of course," I echoed drily. "Where are we supposed to start looking for this thing?"

"A satellite traversing the Scablands picked up an image which they deduced is the correct mechanoid. They believe it is hiding in an old orbital probe that crashed on a small moon."

I plopped my boots on the floor and rubbed my hand against my pant leg. "All right, this can't be worse than that ticket where we had to travel to that Dyson sphere."

"As usual, you have more than enough optimism for both of us," she said. "I'll change our flight plan with your approval."

"Approved. Let's go get this droid."

Seven weeks later, once we reached the Scablands, I realized my optimism may have been a touch inflated.

"Wow, this system is in serious need of a recycle-reuse-refurbish-rewhatever program," I said. Every planet, moon, and asteroid we passed so far in this system, including the space in between, was littered with junk.

"It's called the Scablands for a reason," Fetch said. "The race that lived in this system destroyed itself as well as much of the indigenous life through endless fighting. Despite the relative ease of traveling here, there weren't enough natural resources to entice new developments, so the system became an unofficial dumping ground by those who don't wish to file forms with the Galactic Oversight Directorate."

"Knowing GOD, who can blame them?" I said. GOD is a race of highly advanced techno-forms who established galactic laws and, more importantly, the galactic hyperlink system for traveling across star systems much faster than even lightspeed.

"Some say this particular moon wasn't reset-tled because it's haunted."

I rolled my eyes. "Now, why did you have to

go and say that? You know I hate haunted houses. What's an entire haunted *planet* going to be like?" I could feel the hairs on the back of my neck rise.

"Our destination is a moon, not a planet, and I imagine you're about to find out what it's going to be like. I've initiated landing procedures," she said.

I'd already donned my hab-suit, though I still held my helmet on my lap. Hab-suits are highly advanced spacesuits that are form-fitting and with a helmet no larger than a motorcycle helmet. I sat back and watched the small moon loom closer as Fetch descended through the heavy atmosphere. Just because it had an atmosphere didn't mean it was breathable. In fact, I've learned that most atmospheres would kill a guy like me in ten seconds flat. This one was no different. Comprised of nearly pure carbon dioxide, with a little bit of nitrogen thrown in, it didn't have the right combination for breathable air even though it was nearly as dense and had about the same pressure as Earth's atmosphere.

The moon didn't get any prettier as we descended. It looked like hundreds of nuclear bombs had gone off here a long time ago and no life came back. It was gray like Earth's moon except this one was a slightly darker gray... and it was a literal junkyard of ships, trailers, and a bunch of contraptions I couldn't even begin to guess. In other words, plenty of places for a rogue mech to hide.

There was enough wind and pressure changes that I could feel the turbulence fight us as Fetch brought us down. After hitting a bump that caused me to almost drop my helmet, I joked, "Whoa. Need a refresher course in landings?"

"The weather system is quite active in the upper atmosphere. I'd like to see you try to land this ship," she said.

I can easily fly this ship if given access to connector ports, Shrike said. That was the nice thing about Shrike—he brought more perks than just being a translator. His merger with my cells led to some changes, with one perk being I no longer needed to wear glasses (a good thing, too, since glasses are hard to come by off-Earth).

I cracked my knuckles. "All right."

"I said that in jest," she said.

"Hey, I wasn't a half-bad gamer back on Earth. Show me the controls, and I bet I could do it."

"Flying a spaceship is slightly different than shooting targets in a videogame."

"I'm not saying I'd do it alone. Shrike will help me. We just need a joystick or connector ports or whatever," I said.

"I'm not letting that technoformic virus anywhere near my connector ports."

I don't like this ship, Shrike said.

"Fortunately, there are no controls for bioforms because even the idea of a bioform flying a ship is both ludicrous and hilarious... and lethally dangerous. Now, be a good little crewmember and sit there *quietly* and see how a proper landing is performed."

I sat there, but I might've let out a curse or two when the ship was hit by sudden turbulence. I ended up clasping my left claw on the metal tubing that ran along the side of my seat to better hold me in place. The turbulence leveled out, and Fetch landed smoothly, as I'd come to expect from her. That was one thing about technoforms —they're consistent.

Lifeforms across the universe are made up of two major branches: bioforms and technoforms. Bioforms are all the naturally reproductive species that includes most alien races. And then there are technoforms which are artificially built species. Just like bioforms include a broad range of life, from snails to humans; technoforms include just as much variety, from ship computers to GOD, the Galactic Oversight Directorate.

"Landing procedure complete. Powering down engines now," Fetch announced.

I unbuckled and stood. "Just put the engines on standby. This is going to be a quick in and out."

"It won't be too quick. We are one-point-two kilometers from the provided coordinates due to uneven terrain. If the mechanoid is still at the same coordinates, it surely chose them for a field advantage," she said.

"It won't matter," I said confidently.

I made my way down a level to the lower airlock. As soon as the inner door closed, I twisted on my helmet and clicked it in place. As soon as the helmet formed an airtight, pressurized seal, the somewhat baggy suit fabric tightened around me like spandex. I double-checked the blaster in my hip holster to verify it had a full charge before tapping the screen on the wall to open the outer airlock door.

Stepping outside into a decent breeze, I found the ground harder than expected. I'd assumed the moon would've been covered in something soft like sand, but this ground was rock-hard. The surface was pelted by holes which I assumed had been from some either gunfire or meteor impacts. Gravel and plastic bits littered the surface. Since I was on a plateau, the wind must've blown all the lighter stuff to the lower elevations. I scanned the area, but jagged rocks at least a hundred feet high blocked portions of my panoramic view. A squarish chunk of debris that reminded me of a pinball machine sat off to my right, but otherwise, nothing seemed out of the ordinary.

I took a few steps forward and found the gravity lighter than Earth's, maybe half as much, which made me feel stronger... maybe strong enough to take on a mech if it didn't want to play nice.

No reputable technoform would live here, Shrike said.

"It's a great place to hide with all this metal everywhere junking up sensors," I replied to the voice in my head, then I said louder, "All right, Fetch. Point me in the right direction."

The HUD (heads-up display) in my face shield lit up a line that curved and disappeared behind a rock. Whenever I turned my head, the line adjusted. It really was the next level up in GPS and would've saved me a whole lot of U-turns since I never fully developed a sense of direction (I blame my dad for that).

I made my way toward the rock. They were interesting stones. Not artificial in nature—just cool, almost like giant, murky gray stalagmites that grew upward from the ground rather than down from a cave's ceiling. I wondered what elements and characteristics this moon had to create something like that. (Then my mind drifted to that scene in *Galaxy Quest* where big rocks joined together and became a monster and... nope, not going there).

I tried not to gawk at the rock too long since I had a job to do, and the mech had to know I was coming. Spaceships aren't exactly stealthy when they come in for landing.

As I walked, I asked aloud, "Your spidey senses picking up anything, Shrike?" I could've thought the question to him, but I found it easier to talk. Especially when I had no one else to talk to except for Fetch.

Too many signals, and your body makes a crappy antenna. You need enhancements, he replied.

"I like me just the way I am," I said, glancing at the prosthetic that comprised my left arm from the bicep on down, and added, "Though I wouldn't mind having all my own body parts."

Challenge accepted.

I stumbled. "Whoa, wait, what?"

Technoformic signal ahead, Shrike replied instead.

I double-checked the charge on my blaster out of nervous habit and took tentative steps around the tall rocks that practically formed a labyrinth.

Where? I thought forcefully.

Ahead came Shrike's reply.

Fetch hadn't said anything or displayed anything new in my HUD, and I was still on track, following the trail she laid out for me. I carefully and slowly weaved through the weird stalagmites until they opened to a small valley of what resembled brown moss. That didn't intrigue me as much as the orbital that had crashed near the center of the moss. It was round, black, and artificial, though the bottom half of the sphere was all busted up from crashing into the surface. It reminded me of a busted-up death star.

"The orbital probe you see marks the last sighting of the mechanoid," Fetch said through my helmet.

Is that where you picked up the signal? I mentally asked Shrike.

Many signals in and around the probe. Too many, he replied.

I didn't like the sound of that. *What do you mean? Like each signal's a robot or just too much static around here?*

I didn't get an answer from Shrike because right then, a big, humanoid mechanoid with a face that reminded me of the exhaust end of a ship's engine, appeared out of *nowhere...* right in front of me. It stepped out of thin air and stood before me, with its laser arm pointed directly at me.

The fiery orange orb inside its face focused on me. "Leave!" it commanded in a metallic voice.

"Whoa, whoa, whoa! Don't shoot!" I exclaimed. "Are you Tyrex-67? I'm not here to hurt you. I'm here to bring you back to your company."

Its face glowed brighter just before it fired. The blast missed my head by mere inches and struck a rock behind me. I fired back, my blaster shot deflecting harmlessly off its silver torso. It took a step toward me and fired twice. A shot zipped by either side of my helmet, and I did what any sane person would do.

I ran.

"Leave!" it roared.

I raced into the outcropping of rocks as the mech's shots hit stones near me. Bits of rock bounced off my helmet and suit as I ran, and I didn't slow down until I reached the ship's door. Fetch, having seen everything I'd seen through my helmet feed, was already opening the outer airlock, and I dove inside. I lay on my back, sucking air but wearing a hab-suit made me feel like I could never get enough. As soon as the outer airlock door closed and the light turned from red to green, I pulled off my helmet and drew in long, deep breaths.

Once I could speak, I asked, "Can he break through the door?"

"Undoubtedly. It's a security mechanoid. However, it has chosen to leave rather than continue its pursuit," Fetch said.

I patted my suit and checked my prosthetic arm. "Geez, I got lucky—the mech's targeting system must be off."

"From what I saw, its targeting system is quite accurate. The mechanoid was intentionally missing you, firing warning shots rather than kill shots, which means there is something wrong with its logic chip. Security mechanoids are not programmed to fire warning shots," she said.

"Well, this one did. Maybe that means it won't try to kill me if I approach it again," I said.

"You want to stake your life on a mech's corrupted logic chip?"

"It's either that or not get paid, and if I don't get paid, I don't eat." I dragged myself to my feet with a heavy sigh. "Why does every job have to turn crappy?"

"Look at the bright side. This is the first time something didn't try to kill you," Fetch said.

"Yet," I added. "This is the first time something hasn't tried to kill me *yet*."

THE NEXT TIME I went out, that dang mech snuck up on me again using that same "illusory portal"—at least that's what Shrike called it. It's basically cool stealth tech that can make its user blend into its surroundings enough that it appears invisible. Remember *Predator*? Exactly like that. I wanted that tech, and I really wished Tyrex didn't have it because it was being a pain in my ass.

I'd made it to the brown moss again when Tyrex did its whole "boo!" appearance that just about gave me a heart attack. This time I was prepared and fired the net launcher I'd found rummaging through the ship's drawers. (I've come to appreciate why my dad was a packrat). The net landed on Tyrex, but it turned its arm in a completely unnatural way and used its laser to cut through the netting.

I scrambled to grab the electromagnetic puck from my pocket. Only after I learned my blaster was useless against a security mech, Fetch decided to tell me about the pucks stashed in a crate in the cargo bay. The pucks work like grenades, but instead of exploding, they emit a targeted electromagnetic disturbance, which screws up anything within several feet of it. It was basically a lightning bolt in a puck.

Fetch was shielded against EMPs, but Shrike didn't even want me touching the pucks. He gave me a migraine as punishment for grabbing one. Even after I promised not to use it unless I was sure I'd be far enough away when it discharged, he still left me with a tension headache. Have I mentioned that aliens are dicks, and alien symbionts are selfish dicks?

As I fumbled around in my pocket, Tyrex moved freed itself from the net before I even had the puck in hand. With Plan B gone to hell, I decided to turn tail and run back to *Fetch*.

This time, however, Tyrex didn't leave after I was safely tucked inside. I stared out of the small, round airlock window at it. "What do you think it's thinking?" I asked.

"I'm a computer, not a psychic," Fetch replied. "What do *you* think it's thinking?"

I shrugged. "Maybe it's trying to decide whether or not it's going to try and break inside to get to me. I think the net kind of ticked it off."

"It allowed you to live. It must have a sweet spot for you," she said.

"Yeah? Well, it's got a funny way of showing it."

Tyrex took a step closer, and I instinctively took a step back from the "face" that looked like it could blow a hole through the hull.

"Leave," it commanded. "I will not go with you." Fetch must've been picking up its voice and playing it through her speakers since I never would've heard it otherwise through the ship's hull.

"Fetch, let it hear me," I said to her before speaking louder, "Your company issued a repo ticket. If I leave, someone else is going to show up."

"Not if you tell them I am not here," it said.

That wasn't going to happen because I needed the money. One way or another, that mech was coming with me.

"C'mon, dude. I'm just doing my job. It's not like I've got a choice," I said.

"And my job was to kill anything my client ordered me to kill. I made a choice. You can, too," it said.

"It's not as easy as that. Unlike you, I've got to eat. I've got a ship to maintain."

"Leave. Take another ticket," it said.

"I. Can't."

"Then you will regret your choice." It turned and disappeared through its illusory portal.

———

On day three, I went out with a reloaded net launcher and an electromagnetic puck. I ventured down the path through the rocks (again) and expected Tyrex to appear in the same spot, but this time it didn't. Everything was silent, but I realized that could've been because my helmet was set on noise canceling. I changed the setting. But even then, I only heard the wind. It must've been gustier today since the blowing sound was coming through my helmet speakers louder than before. It didn't feel any breezier, but without trees, it was impossible to gauge wind speed. As I listened, the wind grew louder. I cocked my head. The wind sounded different—it practically buzzed. Then I realized it *was* buzzing.

I snapped a quick three-sixty. I didn't see anything until I looked up to discover a black swarm descending toward me.

"Oh, crap." I took off running back to my ship. As I sprinted, I said, "Fetch, I thought you said there wasn't any life here."

"I detect no life, but I do detect electronic noise," she replied.

I hazarded a glance to find the swarm closing the distance. Hundreds of large, gray wasps zoomed toward me. The nearest wasp shot a laser from a tiny gun mounted on its belly. The shot didn't cut through my hab-suit, but it was strong enough to give an electric shot.

"Ow!"

Three more shots from three other wasps quickly followed. Shrike cursed in his alien language in my brain as I cursed aloud in English. "Stupid, freaking, dang, ow, bug, son of a—!"

The entire swarm was right behind me. They took turns shooting me, and every shot was a sting through my suit. Fetch was opening the outer airlock as soon as the ship was in sight.

"Please try not to bring any of those drones in with you," Fetch said.

"I'll try not—ow! Stop it, you dang—ow!"

The stings motivated me to run as fast as I could. The outer door was only halfway up by the time I reached it. I dove through the opening, sliding across the floor and smashing against the inner door.

Stupid brainskin trying to get me killed, Shrike complained loudly enough that it made my head throb.

"Stop it," I said.

"You want me to stop the door?" Fetch asked.

"No! Shut the door as fast as you can!" I jumped to my feet to face the swarm head-on, but the wasps had stopped right outside the door. They hovered, buzzing angrily in the thin atmosphere, but they didn't shoot. I might have stuck my tongue out at them thinking I was safe, but one wasp apparently took my insult personally and just before the door closed completely, it zapped me in the center of my chest.

"Asshole," I muttered.

Asshole, Shrike echoed, but the way he said it made me wonder whether he was talking about the wasp or me.

"I believe it's safe to assume Tyrex-67 was in control of those drones," Fetch said.

"You think?" I said dryly.

"Yes, I do," she said.

You'd think artificially intelligent computers would understand sarcasm after a few thousand years of evolution, but nope. And I've learned there's a direct correlation between sarcasm and a sense of humor because humor was another thing AI machines struggled with (even though they'll tell you differently).

I twisted off my helmet so I could tug down my suit to find my skin dotted with little red burns from being stung. "Who in the world ever came up with the idea of giving wasps blasters?"

"Insectoid mechs were first used in warfare by the Leptharans in the Torgian Conflict in the fifty-seventh epoch of the common era. In that war, they had proven quite adept as distracting an enemy," Fetch said.

Wrong. Insectoids were used by 111 long before the Torgian Conflict, Shrike said.

Shrike was a 111, and I thought 111 was the weirdest name for an alien race, but I guess it made sense since Shrike was a technoformic goo rather than a bioform like me. Shrike was basically a type of computer, and his language was made up of numbers rather than words.

"Doesn't matter when someone got the idea to give a wasp a blaster," I said. "What matters is that there's no way I'm going back outside with those things buzzing around out there."

"You must go back outside," Fetch said.

"Will not," I said.

"You will because you left your net launcher outside. I doubt you can restrain Tyrex-67 long enough to deliver the electromagnetic puck without a net," she said.

I glanced around me and realized I must've dropped the launcher sometime while I was running back to the ship. "Crap."

"More importantly, you must go back outside to retrieve Tyrex-67. You received a message from Totty. She demands a status update."

I grumbled. "Tell her I'm working on it."

"I do not anticipate that update will improve her mood," Fetch said.

"I don't care about her mood; I care about not dying," I countered.

"You're certainly petulant today," she said.

"Try getting zapped a few hundred times by murderous wasps with guns."

"If you noticed, Tyrex-67 programmed the drones to scare you off, not kill you. I don't believe you're truly in danger. Therefore, I recommend you venture outside and track your target."

We should leave. These mechanoids offer no value. Jack, your handler, offers far more value, Shrike said.

"I'm never calling Jack, Shrike," I said.

A bolt of agony shot through my brain, sending me to a knee.

"Frank, you are in distress. What is wrong?" Fetch asked.

I gritted my teeth and stood. "Nothing. Just Shrike throwing a temper tantrum."

Because you are a dumb brainskin, Shrike said.

"Quit calling me that," I scolded. "Don't forget, I'm the only reason you're not dead."

And I saved your life. We are even, Shrike said.

"A symbiont would never hurt its host," Fetch said. "This is further evidence that Shrike is a virus rather than a symbiont."

Fetch is dumb, Shrike said.

"Play nice," I said to both.

I'd mistakenly freed Shrike from his holding canister in an abandoned Dyson sphere. The cabinet holding him had been marked with a bold red cross, which I'd assumed meant first-aid. But, evidently, in the common galactic language, red crosses denote danger. I had, in fact, strolled right into a quarantined room, and freed something that the original occupants of the sphere clearly didn't want freed. And now the gooey green jellyfish was inside me, interlaced with all my cells. I still wasn't fond of the idea of having some alien symbiont inside me, but he'd kept me alive when I would've died, so I figured he couldn't be evil... or at least *too* evil, right?

Shrike didn't seem too fond of being inside me, either. Evidently, his race preferred to inhabit technoforms and not just any technoforms would do. They needed to be a living, "natural" technoform, which ruled out AI computers like Fetch or mechanoids. There were a lot more bioforms in the universe than true technoforms—evidently, we're a lot faster at reproducing.

Jack, my GOD handler, was the only technoform I'd met, and Shrike was chomping at the bit to transfer into Jack. But since Shrike had already meshed with all my cells, I'd pretty much die an excruciating death if he decided to leave me. Needless to say, I don't plan to touch Jack or any other natural technoform *ever*. Shrike might have acted like he was unwillingly stuck inside me, but he was the one who'd slithered inside me without an invitation. He needed me for environmental protection since his gooey state could only survive outside a host in some weird gaseous atmosphere like the one in his home system. I was stuck with him and planned to keep it that way since I preferred to stay alive.

"If you have recovered, I have news from Totty," Fetch said.

"And what's that?" I asked.

"She wasn't impressed with your status update. On a positive note, she didn't threaten to kill you for failing this time."

I smiled. "Aw, I think she's starting to like me."

"Instead, she mentioned the financial implications of you violating your contract. She specifically pointed out one of those implications: she can repossess this ship should you fail to fulfill your contractual obligations," she said.

I winced. "Oh, now that's just hitting below the belt."

"Since I'd prefer not to be repossessed, I recommend you complete this ticket, the sooner the better," Fetch said. "The insectoids have departed, although I recommend you take a different route this time. I think Tyrex-67 has your current route well and truly surveilled. I will display a new route based on the lowest amount of electrical noise."

I huffed and checked to make sure I still had the electromagnetic puck. "Yeah, all right. I've got this. Heading back outside now."

As I secured my helmet, Fetch opened the door. I regretted not coming up with a better excuse for Totty. Worse, Tyrex was right: I was really beginning to regret my choice to stay.

4 / OLD DOGS, NEW TRICKS

I MEANDERED around rocks and scrap metal for over an hour. Fetch's new route to Tyrex's hideout led me to what I would loosely classify as a junkyard since it looked like a ton of stuff had been dumped here. An old spaceship lay on its side, split in half. Debris was scattered everywhere. Beyond it, another spaceship had barreled into the surface, and it'd broken apart like Humpty Dumpty, and just like Humpty Dumpty, there was no way that ship could ever be put back together again.

There were chunks of debris everywhere and sections of at least two other ships. Since the hulls were the same color and size, I figured they'd all been dumped here at the same time by the same company. If I had extra time after collecting Tyrex, I'd check out the junkyard more, but I doubted I'd find much of value to resell. Chances were every wreck in this system had been fully stripped before getting dumped. Capitalism isn't unique to Earth: capitalism is alive and well across the universe.

I tripped over a piece of ship hull protruding

from the ground and landed on my hand and knees.

Clumsy brainskin.

"Will you quit calling me that, you slimy little hitchhiker. Geez." I started to stand but stopped when a piece of metal—darker than the rest of the junk—caught my eye. It was tucked inside some wreckage and didn't have the coat of dust that dulled everything else. I never would've seen it if I'd been standing. I stood and made my way over to the wreckage. Hidden beneath several sheets of hull was a courier drone. The manufacturer of courier drones must've been one of the richest companies in the galaxy, because every drone looked the same, and they were everywhere. I had four sitting in my cargo bay right now as Totty had me pick up extras at waystations every time I got down to only one drone. Drones were the most convenient, cheapest way of getting anything from one place to another. Basically, they were the Postal Service on a galactic level.

"Huh, how about that," I said. "Fetch, what do you think the odds are this drone would belong to anything *other* than Tyrex?"

"I would place those odds exceptionally low," she replied.

"That's what I'm thinking, too." I figured Tyrex had traveled via courier drone. A robot wouldn't need a full ship like I did. After all, that was how I was planning on returning Tyrex to its corporation.

Did I feel guilty going after a robot that didn't want to be repo'd? Sure, who wouldn't except for a nasty Calcar. But Tyrex was a robot—even with a millennia of circuitry evolution, I wasn't convinced robots had feelings. I mean, Fetch was great at faking it (so was my ex-girlfriend). But from what I'd seen, Fetch's "feelings" seemed to fall perfectly in line with her self-serving tendencies.

Shrike, a natural technoform, was wildly different than the average technoform. He'd thrown enough temper tantrums that I had no doubt he had emotions. Too bad he had the emotional maturity of a two-year-old.

A sound snapped my gaze up to find a small robotic dog peering down at me from where it rested on a beam. It was gray metal with round golden eyes that seemed curious rather than aggressive. Without fur, it reminded me of those hairless dogs down in Mexico—that breed with the hard-to-pronounce name.

I spoke in a soft, higher-pitched voice, "Oh, hey there lil guy. What're you doing around here? Are you lost?"

Danger, Shrike warned.

"It's just a little puppy."

Mechanoids don't age that way.

"Why would someone make a puppy if it wasn't for cuteness?" I asked.

To lure dumb bait.

"I'm not—oh."

Pairs of golden eyes lit up around me from every nook and cranny of the wreckage. There must've been at least a dozen of them stalking me, and each of them were at least three times the size of the puppy. Unlike the puppy, these didn't look curious—they looked very, very hostile... and *hungry.*

"My sensors are picking up a flurry of electro-magnetic activity, Frank," Fetch said.

"Yeah, I kinda got that already," I said in a low voice.

The puppy gave a happy yip before bounding off.

I backed slowly away from the wreckage. I'd only moved a foot or so when I heard a growl behind me. I spun to see two more robotic dogs jumping out of another wreck and taking slow steps toward me, their heads low. It seemed superfluous for the dogs' maker to give them mannerisms of wild dingoes. If the maker was going for scary, they'd definitely accomplished their goal.

I didn't want to stick around to ask. I spun and sprinted forward. Out of the corner of my eye, I glimpsed the dogs giving chase, and they were *a lot* faster than me. I'd never reach my ship in time. I scanned the junkyard as I ran.

Safety to your right, Shrike said.

I made a hard sidestep to miss a dog leaping at me. The dogs were here, there, and everywhere, cutting off my escape route. I raced towards what resembled a giant-sized top-loader washing machine. The contraption was on its side, and its cover stood open. With dogs closing in, I bent and jumped inside and yanked at the cover. It was twisted and didn't want to move, despite me pulling at it with both my hand and claw. I almost had it closed when the first dogs reached me. If I was lucky, the dogs would smash the cover closed in trying to reach me. But I'm not lucky, and robo-dogs are evidently pretty smart. The dogs slowed in time to keep from barreling in, and they went for my hand instead. I instinctively yanked my hand to me but continued to hold the cover as tightly as I could with my prosthetic arm to keep the dogs from pulling it open with their teeth.

The dang dogs went after my prosthetic arm. A dog bit down on my forearm, its metal teeth slicing through my suit and the composite metal beneath. My HUD displayed warnings as it attempted to auto-seal around the teeth. The dog dug in and yanked at my arm with a rhythmic tugging motion while the pack gathered around it.

"Use the EMP puck, Frank," Fetch said.

I fumbled in my pocket for the small puck, which was proving to be an exceptionally hard task given a large dog was trying to yank my arm off. I managed to get a hold of the puck and was just about to tap the timer when the dog yanked my arm off, taking the suit's sleeve with it. The puck, not yet activated, went bouncing through the opening and onto the ground outside and out of my reach.

The suit auto-sealed within a second, exactly like it'd done the last time I lost my left arm (the artificial one, not the real one—losing the real one hurt a lot more). Outside, the dogs tore apart my prosthetic until it was busted up beyond recognition. I groaned. "C'mon, really?"

It was a galactic impossibility that I'd ever be able to repair that arm. One dog had even swallowed the claw, and I winced. If they could do that to something made of metal and hard composite material, flesh would be like Jell-O to the beasties.

I eyed the puck, which had rolled a full two feet from my little hidey hole. I got on my knees to reach for it when the entire pack turned their attention from their now-demolished toy to the juicy treat waiting in the broken washing machine. Dogs lunged at me, nipping at the bent cover, but their teeth slipped off the evidently stronger metal. One finally got a good grip and began tugging the cover open. I tried to grab the door, but every time I did, a dog lunged to bite my arm.

"Fetch, do something!" I yelled.

"I'm a ship with no weapons. What exactly would you like me to do?" she asked.

"Something!"

I glanced at the puck which was now being sniffed by one of the dogs. I unholstered my blaster. Another dog's fervor bent the cover until its head could squeeze through. Metal jaws snapped at me, and I fired point-blank at its head. The dog paused momentarily, seemingly surprised I'd shot it and then shrugged it off, resuming its attack. It shoved its head in deeper, and I kicked it over and over even though my actions didn't seem to make it reconsider. It pushed in deep enough that I knew I was done for when it shook its head and yanked away.

I glanced at the dogs, which were all shaking their heads and running off, yet there were no sounds of scurrying or barking. I noticed then that my helmet's external microphone had been muted. Before I unmuted it, I said, "Was that you, Fetch?"

"You told me to do something, and so I did," she said.

"What'd you do?"

"I broadcast a frequency that would be considered painful to most lifeforms. I gambled that it would be detrimental to their hearing sensors as well. I recommend you return to the ship as the dogs can likely adjust their own sensors."

I did as I was told and ran. It seemed like I was a doing a lot of running on this moon. At least there were no signs of the dogs on the trip back. No sign of Tyrex either, and I was getting really annoyed with it playing hardball.

Fetch opened the airlock and once I was inside, she said, "I see you lost your arm. Again."

I flipped her the bird.

5 / FORTUNE FAVORS THE BOLD

"I NEED A NEW PLAN," I said as I itched the nub of my left arm. It'd been oddly itchy for the past day. Even the skin looked less pink, and I wondered if I picked up some kind of bacteria or something in that brief second my suit had been breached.

Leave this moon, Shrike offered.

"That's not a plan, Shrike; that's defeat," I said as I took a fresh bowl of gruel from the food station (I called it the foodie). After over a year of eating this crap, I'd grown used to it, but I never enjoyed it. I still craved pizza... and steak... and bacon (especially bacon), but I knew even if I could have them, they'd taste bland in space because *everything* tasted bland in space. Fetch said it was because of low gravity and sinuses never quite clearing properly. I wondered if it was something about the constantly recycled air, but whatever. Gruel was better than nothing—after having gone without food for nearly a week before, I'll take gruel any day.

I was on my third bowl of recipe #7, one bowl more than usual. I figured I was burning a lot more energy than usual by running for my life (twice) so eating extra made sense.

"I wonder if the hounds were under Tyrex-67's control. If so, I'm surprised it hasn't allowed anything on this moon to kill you yet," Fetch said.

I guffawed. "What?! Did you not *see* those dogs? I was about to become their new chew toy."

"I saw them as well as the puppy you thought was 'cute.'"

"Well, it was cute for a mech," I said.

"And I saw that any one of those mechs could've easily taken you down before you reached the lavatory reprocessing unit. And even once you were inside, they were playful more than aggressive."

"Is that what you saw? Because believe me, that's not what I saw. And wait a second. What's a lavatory reprocessing unit?"

"It's the unit that recycles waste into usable resources. You sought shelter in the collection drum," she said.

I lowered my bowl, my appetite instantly gone. "I was sitting inside a giant toilet bowl?"

"If you're using a comparison to a general lavatory system, you were sitting inside the septic tank," she corrected.

I sniffed myself. I'd rubbed against alien poop. The thought was not comforting and now my nub was itching. What alien bug had I exposed myself to?

"Tyrex-67 clearly directed the other mechs to frighten you rather than to harm you."

"'Harm' is a subjective word. I still have burn marks covering half my body no thanks to those wasps' lasers, and don't forget, those dogs tore my arm off!"

"Semantics aside, I believe Tyrex and its technoforms do not wish you direct harm. That can play to our advantage," she said.

They're science projects more than technoforms, Shrike said.

"You're just being ornery," I said.

"Shrike's just being Shrike again, I suspect," Fetch said even though she couldn't hear anything he said. I think she could pick up a different intonation in my voice or something when I talked to him. She didn't like him because she was convinced that he was a virus rather than a symbiont. He didn't like her because she was an artificial technoform rather than a natural technoform. For example: he thought she was dumb; she thought he was an asshole. The pair were like teenage siblings. Asking them to get along would be as futile as resisting the Borg.

And I wasn't convinced either one of them had my best interests at heart.

"So what can I do to get to Tyrex so we can get off this rock?" I asked. I was getting tired of Tyrex *not* trying to kill me.

"My recommendation is to attempt discourse," Fetch said.

Dumb, Shrike said.

I didn't relay that comment to Fetch.

"So... what? You want me to just walk up to it?"

"Every attempt to sneak up to it has failed. And despite you being the aggressor, it has not tried to kill you. So, logically, it makes sense to directly approach it," she said.

I frowned, not quite sure I agreed with her. "Is that how my dad would've done it?"

"Your dad would've given up after the first attempt. He made far more money by reselling junk than from repo tickets."

"Why am I not surprised," I said drily.

"Whatever you do, I recommend you do it soon as Totty is growing quite restless about having an open ticket. It hurts her monthly numbers," Fetch said.

"All right, fine. I'll give your plan a shot since you're so sure Tyrex isn't trying to kill me." I popped the bowl into the cleaning station. "But first, I need to take a shower and get the alien poop germs off me."

"You were wearing a hab-suit, which has already been cleaned," Fetch said.

"As you've pointed out on multiple occasions, the human brain isn't fueled by logic," I said.

A truer statement has never been made, Shrike said in one of his more eloquent comments. I chose to ignore him and focus on washing up instead.

I called it a shower out of habit even though I didn't have a shower, let alone a bathtub, on my ship. I had a sink, which meant the only way of cleaning myself was, well, think birdbath. It sucked. I had a cleaning station for clothes and tools, but nothing for me. Someday, when I made enough money to afford one, I was going to install the best damn shower a spaceship had ever seen.

As I freshened up, I paused on my left arm. I could've sworn it looked different somehow, and the coloring was unmistakably off. The nub used to be a pink and white scar. Now it had a greenish hue. "Uh, Fetch, can you run a medical scan on my arm? I think I picked up something when those dogs tore off my arm."

Your arm is fine. I'm working on it, Shrike said.

I jerked. "What do you mean, 'you're working on it?'"

"Are you speaking to the virus?" Fetch asked.

"I'm talking to Shrike," I clarified.

You asked me to experiment with your left arm, Shrike said.

I chortled. "I think I would've remembered something like that."

You did. You said you wanted to have all body parts, and I told you I accepted the challenge. I am working with your cells to build an arm.

"You can rebuild my arm?" I asked.

It's a possibility that I can build you an arm. Terrans can't regenerate, so it wouldn't be your arm, obviously. That idea is stupid.

I frowned. "Then what are you building?"

I told you. I'm building an arm. Dumb brainskin.

"The medical scan has been completed. I detected no new pathogen or infection... other than the alien virus already inside you," Fetch said.

"Shrike says he's building me an arm, or at least he's trying. He's not sure he can do it," I said.

"The difference between a virus and a symbiont is that a symbiont does nothing to its host's body without full approval while a virus does whatever it wants, whenever it wants, however it wants," Fetch said.

"Shrike has my approval." Sort of. "Anyway, I don't have my prosthetic arm anymore, so I guess

I can't complain if he can do something about it."
And it was about time he chipped in for a change.
Sure, he kept me alive by constantly repairing
radiation damage to my cells and strengthening
all my innards against low-gravity loss, but I
didn't think about those things much—they were
kind of like the computer programs that run in
the background. Necessary but not flashy like
Baldur's Gate 3.

"Terrans are an incredibly naïve race," Fetch
said.

"Not naïve. Optimistic. Two very different
things," I said as I began putting on my hab-suit.
"Take for example, it's optimistic of me to walk
right up to Tyrex and offer to chat, all the while
hoping it doesn't kill me or sic his pets on me."

That's idiotic, not optimistic, Shrike said.

"I wasn't talking to you." I snapped my
helmet into place, checked the charge on my
blaster.

I made my way to the lower airlock and
glanced upward before stepping outside. "All
right, Fetch, I'm trying it your way. But if I get
killed, my spirit's coming back and haunting you
forever and ever. Doesn't matter if you believe in
ghosts or not—I'm haunting your circuit boards."

"As a matter of fact, I've met several ghosts.
They are a rather intriguing and gentle race from
the Starrii system."

"You mean to tell me there are alien ghosts
out there?" I asked.

"There is a race with the attributes you relate
to ghosts," she replied.

I shook my head. "Well, I'll not only be a
scary ghost, but also a vindictive one. I will haunt

you!" I gave her an evil laugh and then I exited my ship.

Fetch could've kept talking to me through my helmet speakers, but fortunately for me, she gave me peace. Instead, she displayed my path on my HUD even though I'd already come to know the area too well.

Now that I was out in the open, I felt like an idiot for listening to Fetch. Those robo-dogs could come back at any moment. I looked up and noticed a single drone flying overhead, which I assumed was how Tyrex was keeping tabs on me.

"Uh, hello. I just want to talk to Tyrex. That's all. I swear it. I won't try to take it in," I said. It was a half-truth. I was still planning on taking the robot—I was just trying a gentler approach this time. The more I thought about it, the more I thought the plan sucked.

The drone buzzed closer, and I winced, expecting to get zapped. It buzzed around my head for a moment before zipping away.

This is boring, Shrike said.

"Better boring than dead."

I made my way through the rocks toward the death star, which I'd become pretty convinced was Tyrex's hiding spot.

As soon I emerged into the valley and the death star came into view, I stopped and called out, "Tyrex? It's Frank. I'm just here to talk."

Nothing happened for several seconds until, finally, a wasp mech buzzed in front of my helmet and then flew toward the wrecked orbital. I assumed it wanted me to follow, though it could've been warning me off for all I knew. I took slow steps forward onto the brown moss. It was surprisingly squishy and slippery under my boots, and I caught myself from falling. Aside from its slippery factor, it'd make a decent lawn. I wondered if the moss could grow on Mars since both worlds had similar characteristics.

Don't like this, Shrike said.

I thought the same thing. If the dogs came after me now, I'd never make it back to my ship in time. I needed to start really reconsidering what Fetch said.

Never trust a ship technosystem. They have only their own interests in mind.

"And you're different how?" I asked under my breath.

We are merged. Obviously, my interests are your interests.

"Obviously," I said sarcastically.

Stop. The moss is wrong.

I glanced at the brown moss but didn't see anything weird. "Wrong, how?"

It moved.

I squinted. "I didn't see anything move."

I continued forward but found my steps sluggish. It was then I noticed that the moss had thickened and climbed over my boots.

"You gotta be kidding me." I turned to get off it, but I was stuck. I reached for my blaster and then the moss moved like a surge of water, climbing up my legs and covering my holster before I could get to my weapon. It climbed my torso, and I struggled to break free. It soon covered my helmet, and seeing the moss up close, I noticed that it was artificial in nature—it resembled a blanket of aphid mechs.

"Fetch, I could use some help here," I pleaded.

"I could attempt to discharge some of your suit's energy," she said.

"Do it!"

I felt nothing but the "moss" on me convulsed. Instead of falling off me, the blanket became thicker and heavier. I found myself knocked to the ground. I couldn't see or feel anything. It was as if I was wrapped in an extremely tight, heavy blanket. I had a sensation of movement, but all I could tell was that I was prone and couldn't move even my pinky.

"That seemed to irritate them," Fetch said. "Let's hope they don't wish to kill you."

"Yeah, let's hope. By the way, Fetch, your plan sucks," I said.

We should've abandoned this ticket.

"I agree with you on that one, Shrike."

"The mech-tarp hasn't tried to penetrate your hab-suit yet, which means it's not trying to kill you," Fetch said.

"I'm in a moss burrito. I'm a little concerned about who's dinner I'm about to become," I said.

"Quit being so dramatic," Fetch said.

"Oh? I'd like to see how you'd handle things if someone wrapped you up in a moss burrito," I retorted.

There was a jostling, and I felt my back on a hard surface. The weight constricting me melted away, and the moss poured off my helmet. Before me stood Tyrex, and it had its laser gun leveled, point-blank, at my face.

6 /   NOW WOULD BE A
       GOOD TIME TO TAKE
       UP A NEW SPORT

I EXPECTED TO DIE. I really did. Instead, Tyrex's forearm opened, and its blaster disappeared inside.

"Talk," Tyrex said.

I pushed myself nervously to my feet. "Um, hi."

If robots were capable of glaring, Tyrex was definitely glaring.

"We got off on kind of a rocky start, so I thought I'd come by to talk things out," I said.

"What sort of trick is this?" Tyrex asked.

"No trick. I just wanna talk. You know, it gets lonely traveling across space alone. Well, I've got my ship, but she's not always the best conversationalist, if you know what I mean."

"Because she is not a bioform, she is not good enough to converse with," he said sarcastically.

I waved my hand. "No, that came out wrong. Technoforms, bioforms, makes no difference to me in having conversations. I just meant that— never mind. Just so you know, she's the one who recommended I come talk to you."

"Are you going to talk, or are you going to actually say something?" Tyrex asked.

I looked at the robot. With its single glowing eye in the center of its face, it was very intimidating. We were inside its death star. Tyrex stood in the center, towering over me. Behind it, the robodogs lounged in various places while the mech-wasps were ensconced into an artificial wasp nest (creepy). They weren't the only mechs. There were all kinds hidden away in this crashed orbital, from little robots on wheels to a large square thing on tracks.

Some looked perfectly harmless. Earlier, I hadn't been able to make sense of why Tyrex had remained on this moon and set up a permanent residence here rather than moving from place to place. If I was on the lam, I'd only stop to resupply. This robot, instead, had stayed despite it being riskier. Things were beginning to make sense.

So many mechs, and all were in various levels of disrepair. Few looked wholly complete. This was a regular island of misfit mechs.

"You live here with all these guys," I said.

"They were dumped, just like I was," Tyrex said.

I stared. It'd never occurred to me that anyone would dump a still-functioning mech. "I don't get it. If you were dumped, then why's your corporation want you back?"

"I survived. Since my model was considered end of life, they dumped my entire unit on Mixren to be melted on the surface. I alone escaped. I was not meant to."

I finally saw Tyrex for what he was—something more than a ticket, more than just a mech. "So, if I returned you to them, they'd destroy you?"

"Of course. But I am not going with you. I am staying here." He gestured to the dozens and dozens of droids around him. "They need me."

With the gentleness in his metallic voice, I could almost hear the unspoken words, *I need them.*

And now I felt like utter crap for trying to take him from his family. As a space repo man, I sucked. I glanced across the faces—or at least, face plates—of the various mechs. Even with smooth metal exteriors, I could sense the feelings beneath them. Before, I'd looked at them as artificial things, but they were as alive as I was. Sure, their emotions and thoughts wouldn't be exactly like mine, but nonetheless they had them.

Technoforms feel, even these primitive attempts at intelligent technoforms have emotions, Shrike agreed.

I get it, I thought, then turned to Tyrex. "I'm going to tell my boss that you escaped when I tried to catch you, and that you're long gone out of this system already. But, going forward, you're going to have to be extra careful about not being seen."

"You can't do that," Fetch said in my helmet.

"Why would you do that?" Tyrex asked a fraction of a second after Fetch's statement.

"Because it's the right thing to do," I said in answer to both.

"I meant that you *can't* do that, Frank," Fetch said. "You received a message from Totty after you departed the ship. She said that since there've been delays in completing the ticket, the corporation opened the ticket to additional reclamation teams. Totty said that an old Calcarian acquaintance of yours from Cosmic Claims Consultants volunteered to work the ticket upon hearing you were the first agent assigned."

I groaned. "Krallix."

"I do not understand your answer," Tyrex said.

I blinked. "Oh, I wasn't talking to you. I was talking to my ship." I winced at him. "And I've got some bad news. They opened up your ticket. There's another agent already on his way here."

"Then I will scare him off."

"He's a Calcar. He doesn't scare off. You'll have to kill him," I said.

Tyrex shook his head which looked strange on a mech. His head swiveled left and then right once. "I cannot kill. I have adjusted my programming toward non-violence."

I guffawed. "Wait a second. You're telling me you're a pacifist security mech? How's that work?"

"It does not work as well as I had hoped. Fortunately, that is why my friends help." To make Tyrex's point, one of the larger robo-dogs gave an impressive growl.

"Yeah, you got some good friends there, but Krallix is a major badass. He's got a railgun on his ship and who knows what he'll be packing for an 'up close and personal' encounter. If I were you, I'd hightail it out of here and fast. That's exactly what I'm going to do. Because if I'm here when he arrives, it'll just make things worse. Krallix is the meanest Calcar out there, and he's got a bit of a grudge against me."

Actually, every Calcar I've ever met wanted me dead, and of all the Calcars I've met, Krallix bore a galactic-sized grudge against me for busting up his ship and not letting him steal my ticket. I might have been the one to steal back the ticket he'd stolen from me. But in my defense, Fetch had been the one to damage his ship, not that Krallix is one for semantics.

"I am not surprised," Tyrex said.

I jerked. "What do ya mean? I'm easygoing."

The small mech on wheels squealed, and all the mechs looked to it as it emitted a series of beeps and tones.

Too late. The Calcar is already in orbit, Shrike said.

I braced to run. "I've got to get back to my ship."

"He will see your departure," Tyrex said. "Hide inside your transport until this is over. The wasps will cast an illusory blanket around your ship."

A hero would offer to help. I ran.

7 / KINDNESS IS CONTAGIOUS (AND DEADLY)

"FETCH, DID YOU GET ALL THAT?" I asked as I sprinted, a swarm of wasps buzzing above my head. Their numbers weren't anywhere near the size of the full swarm, but there were enough of them to make me flinch whenever I caught one in my peripheral vision.

"I did. I have prepared the launch sequence but will hold off on starting up the engines, so we won't be noticed by his ship's scans," Fetch replied.

The airlock stood open by the time I reached it. Panting, I impatiently waited for the outer door to close and the inner door to open, then I rushed up the ladder and to the cockpit on the central level. I didn't twist off my helmet until I sat down. "How's it looking out there?" I asked.

"*Star Claimer* is descending through orbit now. Its railgun is aimed at Tyrex's orbital probe, which I believe makes it safe to assume that Tyrex's wasps are doing a sufficient job at casting an illusory blanket over this ship," Fetch said.

I cringed. "You don't think Krallix is going to shoot them all, do you?"

"I think we're about to find out," she said.

I watched in dread as *Star Claimer* descended and then settled onto the moon's surface. The ship bore deep scars from when *Fetch* had rammed its engines (twice). The engines appeared to have been fully repaired, and I considered sneaking out and sabotaging them while Krallix was chasing Tyrex. That way, Krallix couldn't chase me. But that also meant that Krallix would be trapped on the surface with Tyrex and his "family," and I shook off the idea.

I breathed easier once *Star Claimer* powered down—it meant that Krallix wouldn't be using his railgun. Only a few seconds passed before Krallix emerged. He wore a hab-suit beneath armor of some sort, which was painted with splashes of dark red over gray. At least I hoped it was paint. He carried a large energy rifle that looked like it'd be uncomfortably heavy to carry yet the Calcar hefted it with ease. He had two hip holsters and what looked like EMP pucks running down his legs where a stripe would be on those old-timey suits. I was jealous of his rig and made a mental note to figure out how to hook up pucks to the outside of my hab-suit.

And, as if all those weapons weren't enough to do the job, Krallix had a battle ax strapped to his back.

"Hey Fetch, deploy Sparrow so we can see what's happening out there," I said, fidgeting in my seat. Fetch's external cameras would show anything happening in the vicinity of the ship, plus, I preferred advanced notice in case Krallix was onto our camouflage.

"Are you sure you want to see what's happen-

ing? I suspect you won't like the outcome between a Calcar and a pacifist," she said.

"That was an order, not a question," I grumbled. For being the ship's captain, I rarely felt
like it.

"It's your sleep that will be ruined, and then I
will have to hear all about it," Fetch said, then
added, "Deploying Sparrow now."

Fetch's smallest drone was about the size of a
songbird, so I named it Sparrow. I hoped Krallix
was so focused on hunting Tyrex that he wouldn't
notice the drone overhead. Fetch had several
other drones as well, mostly needed for con-
ducting hull repairs while in flight. She never said
why she had Sparrow since all I could figure out
it was good for was surveillance. The drone was
listed as a ship part, so it wasn't something my
dad had picked up along the way. Maybe it was a
drone included in the basic ship package. I decided to ask.

"Hey Fetch, why does a ship need a spy
drone, anyway?"

"Sparrow is not a spy drone. It is the perfect
size to travel through lines and into the smallest
spaces of this ship. It can then identify problems
and make repairs," she replied.

I rubbed my hair. It needed to be washed.
"Oh, I guess that makes sense."

"You really thought Sparrow was a spy drone
even though I am a transport rather than a security vessel?"

I shrugged. "Drones that size in movies were
always spy drones."

"Oh, Frank. There's much more to the galaxy
than what you see in movies," she said.

A screen went from black with green text to a black and white video feed showing the area outside the ship.

A person might think spaceships are high-tech, and they are in a way. But they're also dirty, beat-up, and well-used. *Fetch* had been built a few *hundred* years ago, and it showed with centuries of scrapes, scratches, and dents, not to mention the analog screens in the cockpit. I think those screens were that way from the get-go. When GOD was building ships, they had no regard for the bioforms that would be transported within the hulls. No ship in the galaxy (at least as far as I knew) was piloted by bioforms. That made any flight controls, screens included, a bit superfluous. GOD built their ships to last, but they didn't build them for comfort. Otherwise, I'd have a shower instead of a single sink on the entire ship.

Sparrow climbed high above the wasps that were somehow casting an illusory blanket so Krallix couldn't see *Fetch*. I don't know why Tyrex offered up some of his swarm—maybe he thought that Krallix would leave if he found nci ther Tyrex nor me on this moon. Maybe Tyrex was just being a nice guy, er, mech.

Fetch's drone zipped over the rocky landscape, slowing once Krallix came into view. The feed was grainy, and Sparrow had to zoom in for us to even see what was happening. The rest of the wasp swarm was stinging Krallix with their tiny blasters, and I laughed, remembering the pain. But then I noticed Krallix wasn't even flinching at the attack as he strode forward. His armor must've been deflecting the energy pulses.

As soon as Krallix stepped out of the rock corridor, the robo-dogs ran out from the orbital and raced toward Krallix. The Calcar raised his rifle and fired, but the dogs anticipated his shots and jumped out of the way without slowing. The dogs must've been running fifty miles per hour. Seeing their speed, I realized that the dogs really had been playing with me when they chased me back to my ship. If they'd wanted to kill me, I never would've stood a chance.

They didn't look like they were playing this time.

The dogs quickly cleared the mossy valley around the orbital. Once they were within a hundred feet of Krallix, the Calcar grew frustrated that his shots kept missing them. He dropped his rifle and then tore two EMP pucks from his suit. He twisted each puck and threw them at the incoming pack. The pucks bounced off the hard ground.

I bolted forward in my seat. The dogs backpedaled and tried to retreat, but they weren't fast enough to outrun an EMP. Both pucks went off within a second of each other, blinding Fetch's drone momentarily with flashes of light. When the video feed cleared up, every dog lay lifeless on the ground. Since the feed was still active, Sparrow was evidently safely above the blast radius.

Sadness plucked at my chest even though I hadn't gotten along with the mech beasts. I'm an animal lover, and mech or not, they were still dogs.

I swallowed. "I can't believe he killed them."

"They are not dead. All mechs have backup

routines built into their systems. However, they will be offline for some time until their backup routines can repair and restart their systems," Fetch said.

"I thought EMPs fried chips," I said.

"Perhaps elementary hardware. While pulses surge through any systems not fully protected against EMPs, any decent design includes an electromagnetic recovery system," she said.

"I'm just glad they're going to be okay," I said.

The air shimmered, and more robo-dogs appeared from a portal. Krallix fumbled for another two pucks and tossed them in the middle of the new pack. Flashes of light blinded Swallow's feed again. This time, when the video refocused, the dogs were still running at Krallix. The Calcar spun and ran, and for how scary and fast Calcars are in close quarters, they aren't very good runners. His sprint was my jog, and he pounded the ground with heavy steps. But he didn't run for more than a couple of seconds. The dogs chased until he slowed, stopped, and turned to face them. He held out his arms as if to embrace the mechs and laughed as he walked toward them.

"Ah, good try, mech, but I studied your model. Illusions is one of your model's defensive measures. Show yourself!" Krallix belted out. He spoke in Calcarian, but thanks to Shrike, I could understand Krallix just fine.

I hadn't known the illusion thing about Tyrex. I guess I should've read up on his model on my way here.

The dogs dissipated just before reaching Krallix.

A moment later, Tyrex stepped out from an

illusory portal, and it was the first time I noticed wasps above his head. They must've been projecting holograms around him just like they did with my ship, and how the illusory portal worked suddenly made perfect sense.

There were enough wasps there to project the robo-dog illusion, too. The wasps were more than annoying little stingers. I bet they could do a great projection TV.

"Leave," Tyrex commanded in his deep, metallic voice. His large blaster protruded from his right forearm.

Krallix laughed again. "That's not going to happen. Your company's paying good money to have their lost property returned."

"If you stay, you will regret it," Tyrex said. He clearly wasn't very good at coming up with original threats.

Krallix reached for his rifle, only to notice it still lay on the ground fifty feet from him. Instead, he grabbed his small blasters. Tyrex fired first, striking the ground near Krallix's feet. The Calcar didn't flinch and instead fired, his shots deflecting off Tyrex's armored body.

"Oh no, Tyrex is only trying to scare him, not hurt him," I said. "That's like bringing a knife to a gunfight."

"But they both have guns," Fetch said.

"I meant that he's basically shooting himself in the foot if he's holding back," I said.

"He hasn't shot himself in the foot yet," she said.

I ignored her. She knew what I meant—she was just being difficult. I wondered sometimes if Fetch's original designer coded some feline traits into my ship, because she seemed to thrive on being difficult.

After seeing his blasters were doing no damage, Krallix holstered his blasters and grabbed his battle-ax. "The ticket doesn't say I need to return you in one piece."

He stalked toward Tyrex who gave up firing at Krallix's feet. The Calcar was clearly unafraid of the blaster fire, which made me think that his armor was also blaster-proof.

The pair met halfway. Krallix swung his ax at Tyrex's neck, but the security mech easily ducked and fired an energy blast from his face. Krallix got knocked back a couple of steps. Tyrex followed up the blast with a slam to Krallix's chest that left a dent in the Calcar's armor. Krallix swung low, trying to sweep Tyrex's legs, and the mech jumped back in time. But Krallix used the swing to catch Tyrex off-balance because he headbutted the mech a split-second later.

Both opponents looked evenly matched in size, skill, and speed. Metal clanged against metal as they fought. Krallix managed to strike Tyrex's hip, causing the mech to favor his other leg in the fight. Tyrex struck another blow to Krallix's armor that cracked the metal, and half of the Calcar's chest shield fell to the ground.

They were amazing fighters, and I realized just how outclassed I was when facing other beings. When Fetch called Terrans "fragile," she wasn't being mean—she was right. I was a goldfish in a sea of piranha.

Watching the pair of expert warriors battle, I asked, "Hey Fetch, do you know someone who could teach me hand-to-hand combat?"

"You must first learn your forms," she said.

"Forms?"

"Stances and moves," she replied. "And I can download guides to help you begin. I would've thought; however, that by watching two superior beings battle, you would've realized that you are simply not capable of sufficient hand-to-hand combat. But instead, you seem to think you can fight like a Calcar overnight. I must say, Terrans certainly are a delusional race."

Ignoring her last comment, I leaned forward as I noticed Krallix was beginning to lag. It made sense. Tyrex was a mech—he wouldn't get tired—so all he had to do was wear down Krallix. In the next move, Krallix swung broadly and missed. Tyrex blasted him in the chest. Without his armor, Krallix ended up on his back.

Tyrex grabbed the chunk of broken chest armor that had fallen earlier, and brought it down to decapitate Krallix, but he stopped just before making contact. "Leave me in peace."

I gestured at the screen and yelled, "You had him. What are you doing?"

Tyrex then stepped away and threw down the broken armor. He turned and disappeared through an illusory portal.

Krallix dragged himself to his feet, strapped his ax to his back, scanned the area, and then tapped the armlet on his left arm.

"Have Sparrow zoom in on his armlet. I wanna see what's on the screen," I said.

The video zoomed in, but it was blurry.

"I can't see what he's looking at. Is he calling for reinforcements?" I asked.

In response, Fetch said, "He has a map displayed. It looks like he's tracking electrical readings on the surface. He must've stored Tyrex's signature when they met."

I was surprised she could deduce that from the pixelated image. Then again, she had a lot more processing power than I had brain power.

Krallix then began walking toward the crashed orbital, stopping to reclaim his rifle along the way. As he approached, the brown moss retreated to the orbital and climbed over the exterior surface until it fully covered the sphere.

"What's it doing?" I asked.

"The likeliest rationale for its action is to provide protection to the inhabitants within. Mechtarps are often used by mining camps and colonies for insulation and protection from the elements," she replied.

Krallix continued his approach, glancing once more at his armlet, before calling out, "I see you in there, mech! You might be able to hide behind an illusion, but you can't hide your electronic signature. Don't make me come in there and get you!"

There was no response.

Krallix raised his rifle and began shooting the moss. It screamed and shuddered. Every shot left a blackened patch, but the moss stayed in place.

A second later, the moss parted to reveal the door, and Tyrex rushed out, his arms in the air, and his own blaster out of sight. "Stop! Stop harming Z44. I will go with you."

I could see Krallix's sneer through his helmet's faceplate. "That wasn't so hard now, was it? Come here. If you try anything, I'll start shooting your tarp again." He chuckled. "Pitiful mechs."

As Tyrex approached, the other mechs peeked out from the doorway, whining and begging him not to go. Tyrex paused to give them a final glance. "You will be safe now." Then he turned back to Krallix.

I rubbed my eye.

"Are you crying?" Fetch asked.

"No," I blurted. "It's just allergies."

"I didn't realize you had allergies."

"They act up every now and then," I said and sniffled.

When Tyrex came to a stop before Krallix, the Calcar tossed an EMP puck at the mech, who caught it. A mech cried out from the orbital. Tyrex opened his hand, with the puck resting on his palm, and he watched it as it blew in a flash of light. I jumped when it did.

Sparrow's video feed cleared up to show Tyrex flat on his back, the fiery "eye" of his face a dull, empty hole. Krallix grabbed Tyrex by his head and began dragging him.

Several mechs emerged from the orbital, following, until Krallix swung around his rifle and fired off several shots. He nicked the mech on tracks, and the rest scurried back inside their home, with Tracks limping behind them with smoke wafting from one of its gears.

I leaned back and stared, deflated, as Krallix easily dragged a mech as big as him back to his ship.

The video feed cut.

"What just happened?" I asked.

"I recalled Sparrow as there is nothing left to see. Krallix will haul his quarry to his ship and depart soon after," Fetch said.

I stiffened, took a deep breath, and then stood. "Leave it out there and send the feed to my HUD."

"Don't tell me you're doing something foolish."

I grabbed my helmet. "I'm not. I'm going to get Tyrex back."

8 / THE OLD BANANA
PEEL TRICK

I ventured outside and headed straight toward Krallix's ship, *Star Claimer*.

Did I have a plan? Not yet.

Was I outmatched? Obviously.

Was I going to live long enough to regret my decision? I doubt it.

I could've turned back but didn't. The wasps continued to camouflage *Fetch*, which meant I could've hidden safely onboard until Krallix left with Tyrex, but I wouldn't have been able to live with myself if I did. Sure, I'd come here to repo Tyrex, but I didn't. Totty would probably add another year to my contract for not completing the ticket, but with eighty-one years (plus six months and almost three weeks, but who's counting) left on my contract already, it wasn't like there was a chance I was going to outlive my service to Starshine Seizure Specialists.

I caught up with Krallix as he was about to drag the security mech onto his ship. I didn't have any larger blasters like he did. I pulled out my small blaster and aimed. I wasn't worried about hitting Tyrex. Both had more than enough armor against a weaker energy weapon like mine. I could've hit Krallix anywhere to draw his attention. Instead, I shot him in the back of the head. The beam deflected off his helmet, and he spun around, his yellow eyes homing in on me instantly. His face, which seemed permanently set in a scowl, morphed into an expression of pure glee.

"*You*," he said.

"Yup. Me," I said, and fired again. This time, I aimed for his partially armored chest but didn't aim carefully enough. The shot tapped him on the shoulder.

"I prayed to all nine gods that you would be here for me to gain my revenge. They did not disappoint me," he said before dropping Tyrex and unslinging his rifle. Unlike him, I wore no armor, so I dove behind a boulder.

He chuckled and then yelled, "Don't worry, soft little flesh bag. I won't kill you with a shot. I plan to take my time killing you, and then I will have you for dinner."

Sometimes, I'd rather not be able to understand other languages.

I glanced over the edge of the rock to see the Calcar tramping toward me. He'd dropped his rifle and now held his ax. I jumped to my feet and took off running. Calcars are famed for their combat skills, but that meant they were overconfident, and I already knew two of Krallix's weaknesses. One, he couldn't run fast; and two, he was easy to piss off.

I glanced behind me to find Krallix drawing his blaster in one hand while still holding the large ax in the other. Evidently, I was putting too much space between us for his comfort.

"Oh, crap." I weaved until I found another boulder. I slid behind it and squeezed off two quick shots the same time Krallix fired. If I could hit his chest—where Tyrex broke Krallix's armor plating—I had a chance at killing him, but my shots went wide. His shot chipped shards from the rock a few inches from my helmet.

"Your ship's looking a bit beat-up over there. Looks like you should take better care of her," I called out.

"It took me four months to bring the engine back online after you rammed it, you acrid piece of rotten meat," he said.

"How about it serves you right for stealing my ticket. Makes me wonder, maybe I should smash your engine again for trying to steal another ticket from me. By the way, what's up with you always going for my sloppy seconds?"

Krallix cursed. "I am going to grind your bones and use the powder to season my soups," he called back.

I chuckled and made sure he heard it because I refused to let him know how scared I was. I noticed he was closing in. Closer for me to get a shot, but unfortunately, closer for him to strike. I fired several shots at his chest, but he'd twisted to the side so that the shots deflected off his arm's plating. I jumped up and sprinted toward the junkyard.

I made it barely twenty feet before I felt a stabbing pain through my left thigh. I stumbled and fell. Krallix laughed behind me. "You are mine, flesh bag."

My suit had auto sealed. Glancing at my leg, I saw there was only a patch for an entry wound, which meant the shot wasn't through-and-through. Still, it felt deep enough, like someone had shoved a hot poker through the back of my thigh. I tried to keep from crying out as I forced myself up and back to my feet.

"Surrender, flesh bag. A security mech couldn't defeat me. You stand no chance," Krallix said.

"I don't suppose you could help heal me, Shrike," I pleaded softly.

That is not the way I work, brainskin. Get up and run. It's a hassle merging with a new host.

I gritted my teeth as I hobbled forward. Krallix was now faster than me, and the only good part about that was he no longer seemed interested in shooting me (again). He'd slung his rifle over his shoulder, though he also had two more blasters readily accessible in hip holsters. And a battle ax which wouldn't pose a threat until Krallix was in swinging range... or throwing range.

Oh, god, could a Calcar throw a battle ax?

I stumbled faster, dragging my left leg. Above us, I saw the swarm of wasps hovering, and I couldn't tell if they were watching the show or waiting for orders. Either way, I supposed there wasn't anything they could do.

Fetch spoke through my helmet then, "Move faster, Frank. At your current pace, Krallix will catch you in eight minutes."

"I'm moving as fast as I can," I moaned. "If you didn't notice, I've been shot in the leg."

Every couple of seconds, I looked over my

shoulder to find Krallix, seemingly quite pleased as he stalked me, definitely closing the distance, ax in hand.

"My first meal of you will be a filet of your heart with a nice blood sauce," Krallix announced. "Although, perhaps I'll start with a roast of your leg, so that you can remain alive to watch as I eat you."

"I recommend more fruits and vegetables in your diet," I said through labored breaths, trying to pretend I wasn't in complete agony and terror.

"Mm, yes, I will definitely start with your leg. I'll keep you alive so you can watch me eat each of your limbs, until all that remains of you is your chest and head which I will use as the centerpiece of my table."

I hated Calcars.

I fired again, and the blast hit the unarmored side of his chest. He grunted and a pained look flashed across his features. I watched as his suit sealed over the wound, but he remained on his feet. He sneered at me. "That was a mistake. You will pay for that."

I fired two more shots but missed. "What, don't like your dinner fighting back?"

Krallix snarled and started jogging toward me.

I ran as quickly as I could, my injury tunneling my vision with every jostle. Krallix had taken a direct chest shot and was still on his feet. Exactly how strong were Calcars? I had been counting on taking him out with that shot. That left me with exactly zilch on being able to take him out on my own.

"Fetch, I need a path through the junkyard to put some space between me and him," I said.

"Sending Sparrow to search," she replied. A few seconds later, she said, "I've identified two potential paths that are too small for Krallix to traverse. But you'll need to be limber," she replied.

"I can be as elastic as Mr. Fantastic if I got to." A map with a line appeared on my HUD. "Got it." Krallix was catching up. It was going to be close.

I glanced back constantly to make sure he wasn't going to shoot me in the back. While it didn't look like he was going to shoot me, he continued jogging after me, his hands twisting hungrily around the ax handle. Evidently, I'd ticked him off enough that he wanted to finish our business up close and personal. Though, if he'd really wanted to eat me, I would've thought that another blaster shot to my legs would keep me fresher than chopping me up with his ax. Then again, Calcars aren't known for their intelligence.

I'd hoped Krallix's bulk would've slowed him down by now, but he seemed single-minded about catching me. My leg hurt something fierce, but my adrenaline was helping tamp down the pain enough that I could continue forward. I managed to pick up speed once I saw the first crashed ship, and I followed the line Fetch laid out on my HUD into that ship.

The ship had lost a large section of its hull when it'd been dropped on the surface, and the ceilings had bowed downward as gravity laid its claim. The line on my HUD directed me under a ceiling that had almost fully collapsed. "You weren't kidding about being flexible," I said as I lowered myself down to the floor. Once I was down, the sharp torment in my leg lessened to a pounding throb.

Krallix barreled into the crashed ship. "Where do you think you're going, little mouse?"

I scurried, kicking with my good leg, to shove through the opening that was well under two feet high. I'd just squeezed through when Krallix brought down his blade, striking the floor where my foot had been a microsecond earlier. I ignored the burst of pain when I yanked my feet to my chest.

Krallix yelled something untranslatable, and I twisted to climb through the mess of bent metal and tangled cables.

"Come back here, you rotten flesh bag!"

"Nope. You didn't ask nicely," I said as I moved as fast as I could, which wasn't very fast at all.

Krallix's ax blade smashed against the fallen ceiling over and over. His blade was so sharp that with every swing, he sliced cleanly through metal. I never looked behind me; instead, focusing on climbing over and around wreckage. By the time I emerged through a hole in the hull, the smashing had stopped. I frowned and looked around to see Krallix standing behind a five-foot-high section of the ship's hull. He was raising his ax, and I bolted to the right just as he brought it down.

I felt the tickle of the blade on my back as it slashed downward, but it hadn't sliced the fabric. I couldn't help laughing until my breath was sucked away when I put weight on my injured leg. Krallix shoved aside the hull and was right behind me. If I gave into pain now, he'd have me.

"I need the fastest route to the misfits, Fetch," I managed to say through clenched teeth.

My HUD's map displayed a new line.

The junkyard wasn't far from the home of the misfit mechs, but it was still a good eighth of a mile over uneven terrain, and that felt like a hundred miles with a bad leg and a pissed off Calcar on my tail.

I kept moving forward, and Krallix kept pace.

"Damn it, turn and fight, you worthless flesh bag," Krallix wheezed when we reached the valley.

"I—don't..." I quit trying to reply. My chest burned and my leg hurt too much to bother with words.

Before us stood the small valley. Most of the dogs were still down, but their legs were twitching. One was shakily on its feet. I ran past them onto the mech-tarp that had resumed laying down again on the ground like brown moss. I slowed after I ran several steps onto it.

Krallix kept running full tilt. He ran onto the tarp, and he grinned maniacally at seeing he caught me. He thought I'd slowed down from exhaustion. He was wrong. He swung his ax in a wide arc to decapitate me, but he lost his footing and flailed as he fell onto his back.

I'd remembered how slippery the tarp was when I first stepped on it. I also remembered how easily it had mummified me. Krallix was strong, but I was gambling that he wasn't stronger than a field of ticked-off brown moss.

He started to get up, but the tarp engulfed his

hands and legs before he could, restraining him in a prostrate position.

I grinned down at him. "You know what they say: all's fair in love and repo."

The mech-tarp continued to weave around him until it fully enveloped the furious Calcar, and I enjoyed every second watching him be trapped by Z44 like I once was. But then the brown moss darkened, and the cocoon around Krallix began constricting. Metal crunched and muffled screams echoed as the cocoon shrunk impossibly smaller. Blood seeped out through the mech-tarp.

My humor gone, I gingerly stepped off the tarp even as I continued to gape. It'd only taken seconds to squish a seven-foot Calcar into a three-foot mess. Once it finished, Z44 relaxed and rolled back out across the ground. All that was left of Krallix was a crumpled tin can of armor and hab-suit, with *stuff* oozing from holes everywhere in the suit.

I like Z44. Reminds me of my kind.

The idea there was something living inside me that enjoyed what had just happened did not comfort me in the least.

I heard movement behind me, and I turned to see the misfits emerge from the orbital. The mech-puppy bound past me and to its pack, of which more were back on their feet. The mechs walked, wheeled, and floated toward me. The mech on tracks that had been injured was now being towed by a smaller mech on tracks. I felt a touch on my hand, and I noticed the moss was gently brushing against my fingers. I tried not to yank back in revulsion, and instead gave it a nod. "You did the right thing."

It rippled as it pulled away, and I got the sensation it just thanked me. I turned to the other mechs. "You're all going to be safe now," I said and then glanced in the direction of Krallix's ship. "Let's go get Tyrex."

THE FOLLOWING DAY, I found the small mech with a bad track plugged into *Star Claimer*'s cockpit interface while Tyrex had a panel open to the right of the console, a mess of wires exposed.

"It's time?" he said without looking up.

"It's time," I replied.

He untangled himself and joined my side, and we made our way through the Calcar's main corridor.

"How is your injury?" he asked.

"It'll heal." I leaned on the metal pipe I was using as a cane. It was heavy but helped me keep the weight off my leg enough to make the pain bearable. "And how're your circuits after the blast?"

"Operating at ninety-three percent," he replied.

We stopped to allow a small mech on wheels to pass. It was carrying what looked like boxes of Calcarian food. In just a matter of hours, the interior had gone from a cluttered mess to a polished sheen.

"You and your buddies look like you'll have this ship ready to go in no time," I said.

"*Star Claimer* itself was no small help. It is quite relieved at having its recall coding removed, and it sees us as a far better crew than serving a Calcar. While I have no doubt Cosmic Claims Consultants will open a ticket to reclaim this ship, we will make sure that there is nothing identifiable on either the interior or exterior by the time we launch."

We stepped through the open airlocks and outside where mechs were busily working on the ship's hull. The identification code, that resembled a QR code, had been removed, and wasps were painting a new code. Z44, having regenerated its damaged bits, was smoothing sharp lines on the hull. The ship, which had once looked aggressive, now looked like a well-worn passenger transport.

Not far from the ship waited a spherical mech that seemed to float in the air like a balloon. As we approached, I said, "I wish there was another way."

The small orb made a series of beeps and tones, and Tyrex responded in like.

Since Shrike had merged with me, I'd been able to understand every bioform's language I'd come across, but I still couldn't understand technoformic languages—I wondered if he was intentionally not sharing that skill with me.

The wasps swarmed down to hover just above our heads.

"Your camera is ready?" Tyrex asked.

"My drone is in the air and recording," Fetch said through my helmet.

"It's ready," I relayed to him.

He looked up at the wasps, and a hologram appeared in the distance. A battle scene was underway between Tyrex and Krallix in front of *Star Claimer*. The illusion looked as real as the battle that had taken place a day earlier. In this scene, Tyrex got the upper hand, and Krallix pulled out a puck—but it was flashing a bright red instead of the yellow color of EMP pucks. A second later, the puck exploded, obliterating Krallix and Tyrex. Instinctively, I crouched and covered my head before I quickly remembered that none of this was real. I stood. As the smoke cleared, a massive hole appeared in *Star Claimer*'s hull, and the ship's landing gear had shattered. Bits of metal were scattered across the ground—all that remained of Tyrex. A few seconds later, the hologram disappeared.

Tyrex turned to me, watching expectantly.

"I'm editing and preparing the video to send now," Fetch said in my ear, then added, "It has been sent, and I've received a delivery receipt."

"It's sent," I said aloud. "Now, we wait."

A full minute passed before Fetch said, "Totty has replied. The company requires physical proof of destruction."

I said to Tyrex, "It's what you expected. They need proof."

He gave a slight nod, and then without hesitation, he lay on the ground.

All the other mechs had stopped their tasks to surround Tyrex.

The orb that had been floating nearby zoomed in. Small pincers and rods emerged from its smooth surface, and it began cutting away Tyrex's limbs.

I winced as an arm was amputated, and I wondered if it hurt or if Tyrex even had pain receptors. We all stood quietly and watched for over an hour as Tyrex was fully dissected. As a body part was removed, a dog would grab it and carry it several hundred feet away, depositing it in a pile. Watching the process was quite disconcerting.

Soon, all that remained uncut of Tyrex was his head and the right quarter of his torso.

The orb beeped and then floated back.

"It is done," Tyrex said.

I stared helplessly at what remained of the security mech that now seemed so fragile. A small mech on wheels whizzed by, drawing my attention. It carried a red puck exactly like the puck used in the hologram. It had been one of the weapons they'd found in Krallix's impressive arsenal. The mech activated the puck, dropped it on the pile of Tyrex's body parts, and then zoomed away at a blurring speed.

Three seconds later, a large explosion rattled the ground. My helmet's external microphone muted followed by a shockwave. I stumbled back a step. Before the dust settled, the dog pack ran toward ground zero.

"Your courier drone is ready?" Tyrex asked.

His question spurred me into action. "It's in my cargo hold."

I limped to my ship as Fetch opened the cargo bay door. By the time I walked up the ramp, a dozen dogs had caught up, each carrying various bits of destroyed mech parts. I opened the lid to the drone nearest the door, and the dogs stood on their hind legs to deposit the parts inside. Within minutes, the dogs completed their job. I closed the lid and saw that Fetch had already inputted the ticket number into the courier drone's shipping panel. The pod then activated, and I stepped away as its small magnetic propulsion engines launched it off the floor and then, like a bullet, it shot out of the cargo bay and into the sky.

As soon as Fetch reported Totty's response, I headed back outside to find the mechs had already returned to their work on *Star Claimer*. I would've loved to have raided Krallix's ship and arsenal for myself, but the misfits needed the weapons and the ship's resources a lot more than I did. If Tyrex or *Star Claimer* were discovered to be still functioning, guaranteed there'd be repo tickets going out for them.

Tyrex had been lifted by a mech that rolled along on what looked like ball bearings. I had to look down on him as his head was raised about three feet from the ground.

I frowned down at him. "You sure your buddies will get you fixed up?"

"They will build me a new body," he replied.

"Good." I felt relieved to report, "It's done. They accepted the drone and closed the ticket. You're going to be safe now." While the drone would travel months to its destination, its internal scanners would've already delivered detailed images of its contents to its recipients.

"Thank you for your help. I owe you for my life and that of my family. Whatever you want, it is yours," he said.

"Just stay safe out there. I don't want to see another ticket for you pop up on my list." I winked at him.

"You will not."

With that, I returned to my ship, whistling a tune. While I was glad to see things work out, I wished that I'd come up with the idea a couple of days earlier. Then, I wouldn't have had a blaster shot to my leg. What matters is that I survived, and *Fetch* is still capable of flying (and this ticket will make a great chapter in my memoir).

"Get us ready for launch, Fetch," I announced as I took a seat in the cockpit.

"Ready to launch upon your command," she said.

"Let's rock and roll."

As we departed the Scablands, I scrolled through the news from Totty. I was relieved to see that she had made full payment for the last ticket. I was less than enthused at seeing she'd sent two more tickets. Zuddlians clearly didn't believe in vacations. I sighed, leaned back, and scratched at my left nub which had begun to itch nonstop.

I rolled up my sleeve to see the nub of my bicep longer and *greener* than it had been. There was fresh skin, but it was a bright lime green. Not a soft green like a Floid's smooth skin. It was the color of the slimy technoform that was living rent-free in my body.

After feeling Shrike's glee at Z44's murder of Krallix, I was beginning to wonder if Fetch had been right about Shrike all along. I noticed my journal lying on the bench seat to my right. I'd thought that Krallix was the villain in my story, but now I was beginning to wonder if Shrike wasn't the real villain all along.

No such thing as heroes and villains; everything is a matter of perspective.

His response didn't make me feel one iota better.

ABOUT THE AUTHOR

Rachel Aukes is the award-winning author of forty novels, including 100 *Days in Deadland*, which made *Suspense Magazine*'s Best of the Year list. When not writing, she can be found flying old airplanes over the Midwest countryside and catering to an exceptionally spoiled fifty-pound lapdog.

Join Rachel's spam-free newsletter to be the first to hear about new releases: www.rachelaukes.com/join

ACKNOWLEDGMENTS

With many thanks to Diane Bryant for making my stuff look good; to the Propellers for being the best damn writing group; to Brian for the hugs; to Ellie for the endless supply of doggie kisses; and to *you* for picking up this story and opening the galaxies within it.